TURKEY

AEGEAN SEA

Seriphos

CRETE

A Ladybird Book
Series 740

Greek legend has many stories of heroes who
battle with monsters and perform impossible tasks
with the help of the gods. Theseus and Perseus
are two of the best known of such heroes, and
the monsters they tackled are frightening
even nowadays.

Since some of the names in Greek mythology are hard
to pronounce, here is how the ones in this book are
pronounced.

Theseus	*Theess-use*	Danae	*Dan-ay-ee*
Aegeus	*Ee-gee-us*	Acrisius	*Ack-ree-see-us*
Poseidon	*Po-sy-don*	Perseus	*Per-suse*
Minos	*My-noss*	Zeus	*Zuse*
Minotaur	*Minno-tor*	Polydectes	*Polly-deck-teez*
Cnossos	*K-noss-us*	Athena	*Ath-ee-na*
Ariadne	*A-ree-add-nee*	Hermes	*Her-meez*
Naxos	*Nack-soss*	Medusa	*Med-yoo-sa*
Seriphos	*Serry-foss*	Pegasus	*Peg-a-suss*
Dictys	*Dick-tiss*	Andromeda	*An-drom-ida*

Theseus and the Minotaur

Perseus and the Gorgon's head

Famous Legends BOOK 1

by J. D. M. Preshous
with illustrations by Robert Ayton

Ladybird Books Loughborough

THESEUS AND THE MINOTAUR

Theseus was the son of Aegeus, the king of Athens, but the story says that his real father was Poseidon, god of the sea.

When Theseus was still a baby, his father left him with his mother in their country house, so that he could grow up safely. This was at Troezen in the east of Greece, about a hundred miles south of Athens, which was a very long journey in those days.

Before he returned to Athens, Aegeus placed a sword beneath a huge, heavy stone.

"When my son is strong enough to lift that stone and take out the sword," he said, "send him to me in Athens, to take his place there at my court."

Aegeus went away and Theseus grew up in the country. Each year he went to the stone to see if he could lift it.

Although Theseus tried hard, it was nearly twenty years before he could lift the stone and take out the sword. At last he succeeded and, saying goodbye to his mother, he set off alone for Athens.

The journey was long and dangerous. He met many robbers and fought and killed them, before he reached his father.

Theseus found his father worried and sad.
"Why should the king of such a great city as
Athens be sad?" he asked. Aegeus explained.

"Across the southern sea," he said,
"there lies an island called Crete. Its king,
whose name is Minos, rules over all Greece.
His navy is the strongest in the world, and
all our cities have to pay him for their
safety."

Aegeus' head was bowed as he told Theseus the story.

"Every year a Cretan ship comes to Athens and takes away to Crete seven of our young men and seven of our most lovely girls. We never see them again.

"They say that in King Minos' palace there is a great maze called the Labyrinth. In this lives a dreadful beast called the Minotaur. He is half-man, half-bull, and he lives on human flesh. Our girls and young men are sacrificed to him.

"Tomorrow the Cretan ship will arrive again. This is why I am so sad."

"Father," said Theseus, "let me help the city. I will go to Crete as one of the seven young men, and I will kill this Minotaur."

Aegeus looked up in horror. No one had ever returned from the Labyrinth where the Minotaur waited.

Aegeus clasped his son to him. "No," he cried. "You cannot go. If I lost my son I should die. Let me hide you away in the palace until the Cretan ship has gone."

Theseus smiled and spoke gently to his father. "I must go," he said. "It is not right that our young men and girls should die like this to please the cruel Minos. I will kill the Minotaur, and return in a ship with a white sail so that you will know the good news more quickly.

"If I should fail and die, I will arrange for the news to be brought to you in a ship with a black sail. But do not be afraid. The gods will help me."

Aegeus wept, but he allowed Theseus to go. So when the Cretan ship came to take away seven young men and seven girls as its victims, Theseus was among them, and he was taken away to Crete.

At last the ship came to the island of Crete and the prisoners were taken to King Minos' palace at Cnossos.

Hearing that the son of the king of Athens was among them, Minos ordered the prisoners to be brought before him. He had heard of Theseus and of his courage, and he wanted to see him. There were few young men who would brave the Minotaur!

He spoke to the hero with cruel pleasure, enjoying the thought that Theseus was to die.

"You are a brave man," he said, "but a fool. Even if you are a king's son, the Minotaur will kill you, or you will be lost in the Labyrinth."

Theseus replied boldly, "You are not fit to be a king. But I warn you that your end is coming. With the gods' help I shall kill the Minotaur and destroy your palace."

Minos laughed loudly and dismissed the prisoners, but his daughter, Ariadne, who had been watching, did not laugh. She found herself thinking of this brave and handsome man who had defied her father. She made up her mind to help him.

She gazed after the prisoners as the guards led them away, and wondered what she could do.

No one had ever escaped from the Minotaur before, but there must be a way! Then she had an idea.

Theseus and his friends were taken to the part of the palace called the Labyrinth. This was a maze of passages so dark and twisting that anyone who wandered into it could never find his way out again. Somewhere in the darkness lurked the terrible Minotaur, waiting to devour them. Ariadne followed at a distance, then slipped quietly up to Theseus.

Before the guards could see, she
whispered, "I am your friend. Here are two
gifts you will need." She pushed two objects
into Theseus' hands and slid away.

When the guards had left the prisoners in
the darkness, Theseus looked at the gifts
that Ariadne had given him. One was a
sword and the other was a ball of wool.

Theseus knew at once what he must do. "Stay here," he ordered the others, "and keep hold of one end of this strand of wool. I will take the other and make my way into the Labyrinth to find the Minotaur."

With the thin lifeline of wool in his hand, he set off to face the terror of the Labyrinth.

Behind him, the others waited fearfully. Would he succeed? One girl was crying and her friends comforted her. "Have no fear, Theseus will save us," they said, although they too were frightened.

Theseus moved cautiously forward, slowly letting the wool out behind him. He groped his way along the many passages, which seemed to twist and turn in every direction.

It grew ever darker as he went further and further into the Labyrinth, and the ball of wool grew smaller.

Theseus knew that the Minotaur could
appear from behind a pillar at any moment.
He must be ready to fight it.

He stopped and listened. There was not
a sound. He felt bewildered and lost. Where
was the Minotaur? Did it know he was in
the Labyrinth? Theseus drew his sword, and
tried to see through the darkness.

As he remembered all the stories told about
the Minotaur, he began to grow frightened.

Only the thin strand of wool saved him
from panic. Even this was running out; it
was not long before he felt the end of the
wool between his fingers. He turned and
began to rewind it.

Suddenly, from behind him, he heard a
terrible snarl which made his blood run cold.
He swung round to see where it came from,
his sword gripped tightly in his hand. He
was ready to battle with the monster.

There was a faint light and he could just see the outline of the Minotaur, like a huge man with the head of a bull. The beast charged and seized Theseus by the throat. But the hero was ready and after a tremendous struggle, he plunged his sword into the Minotaur's side. With a fearful bellow the creature fell dead. It would trouble the world no more.

Now Theseus had to find his way back through the maze. Although it was still dark, he was no longer afraid. The Minotaur was dead, and all he had to do was follow the wool back to where his friends awaited him. They rejoiced to see him, and asked many questions about the Minotaur.

Then Theseus and his friends overpowered the surprised guards and fought their way out of the palace, setting parts of it on fire as they went. Ariadne went with them.

The palace of King Minos of Cnossos was burning, and the king's cruel reign was at an end.

No longer would the sacrifice of seven youths and seven maidens be demanded from the king of Athens every year, for the Minotaur was dead.

Theseus was sailing back to his home in triumph.

On the way back to Athens, the vessel stopped at the port of Naxos. The youths and maidens, together with Theseus and Ariadne, landed to look at the beautiful island.

Ariadne strayed apart and fell asleep. Theseus had grown tired of her, so he summoned his companions and they sailed on, leaving her alone on the island.

The gods punished Theseus for his base action by making him forget to change the sail on his ship to a white one, as he had promised his father to do.

Back in Greece Aegeus was waiting for his son's return. Every day he would sit on a high cliff overlooking the southern sea, and watch for a ship sailing in from Crete.

At last he saw a speck on the horizon. Slowly it turned into the shape of a Cretan ship. Aegeus cried out in grief, for the sail that billowed above the painted hull was black. His son must be dead.

Running forward, he hurled himself over the cliff and fell to his death in the sea.

Unaware of this, Theseus sailed triumphantly into the harbour of Athens. Soon he became king, but he could never forgive himself for causing his father's death.

PERSEUS AND THE GORGON'S HEAD

In the Aegean Sea, between Greece and Turkey, there are many islands. One of these is called Seriphos.

One day, Dictys, a fisherman of Seriphos, was walking along the beach near his home. He was surprised to see a large chest at the edge of the sea. The waves were lapping against it.

He pulled it slowly, little by little, on to the sand, away from the sea. It was very heavy. Then he stood looking at it, almost afraid to open it. What could be inside?

Dictys hoped there might be treasure in it, for he was a poor man. At last he plucked up courage, and raised the lid. He was filled with amazement.

A beautiful girl looked up at him, and in her arms was a baby!

The girl was called Danae, and she was the daughter of King Acrisius. A prophet had told Acrisius that his grandson would kill him, and Acrisius had locked Danae up in a tower of brass so that she could not get married and have children. In spite of this, Zeus, king of the gods, had married her secretly.

Then Acrisius was told that Danae had given birth to a son, and he was frightened. He did not want to kill Danae, so he had her and the baby put into a chest and had them cast into the sea.

When Dictys opened the chest and found them he took them to his hut and looked after them.

The baby grew into a strong young man. His mother called him Perseus. She always said that his father was Zeus, king of the gods.

The king of Seriphos was Polydectes.
He was a cruel man and all the people of
the island feared him.

When he met Danae, who was very
beautiful, he fell in love with her. He wanted
her to marry him, but Danae had heard of his
cruelty and she refused. She did not really
want to marry anybody, because she was
quite happy.

One day Polydectes held a feast, to which he invited all the nobles of the island. He invited Danae as well, so that he could spread his riches before her and persuade her to marry him.

The young Perseus too went to the palace. He was not invited, but he slipped in amongst the crowds. He wanted to protect his mother from the king, for he knew she feared him.

During the feast, Polydectes turned to Danae. "Come, my love," he said, smiling. "Let us make this our marriage day for all to see. If you will be my queen, you shall have all that your heart can desire."

Danae shook her head. "I am content, Polydectes, and do not wish to marry again," she replied.

The king still smiled, though he was becoming angry.

Then Perseus stepped forth from the crowd and spoke boldly. "My mother does not wish to marry you, O King. Let her live in peace."

The king's eyes blazed with anger. He knew he could never win Danae for his wife so long as Perseus was there to protect her.

"Danae may live in peace if you will accept a challenge," Polydectes said cunningly.

"Are you brave enough?" he asked.

Perseus nodded. The king laughed in triumph. "Then I challenge you, Perseus, to bring me a Gorgon's head!"

Perseus stepped back in horror. He was trapped. He could not refuse, but how could he bring back a Gorgon's head? He left the palace with the laughter of Polydectes ringing in his ears.

There were three Gorgons. Once they had been beautiful women but they had boasted about their beauty. The gods had punished their vanity by turning them into hideous monsters. They had bronze wings, clawlike hands, tusks for teeth and snakes for hair. One look into a Gorgon's eyes would instantly turn a man to stone!

Perseus walked sadly away from the palace. How could he find the Gorgons and kill one of them? He knew that Polydectes was sending him to certain death.

Suddenly there was a blinding flash of light. Then he saw that there were two figures standing before him. One spoke:

"Perseus, we have been sent by your father Zeus to help you. I am Athena, goddess of wisdom, and this is Hermes, messenger of the gods. Take these gifts and travel northwards until you come to the sea. There you may seek help from the three Grey Sisters."

In another flash the figures were gone.
Perseus eagerly looked at their gifts – a
sharp, curved sickle, a bright, polished shield,
a bag to hang from his shoulder, a cap, and
a pair of winged sandals. With such help
from the gods, surely he must succeed
in his task!

Perseus found that with
the magic sandals he could fly.
With the cap on his head, he was
invisible. With new hope he flew north
over the mountains of Europe, on his way
to find the Gorgons.

He flew for a long, long time, and at last came to the shore of a dark, misty sea. He did not know where he was, nor where to look for the Gorgons.

Then he saw the Grey Sisters on the beach below. They were old and ugly — with only one eye and one tooth to share between them. They were the only people who knew where the Gorgons lived, and they would not tell Perseus the way.

Putting on his cap, Perseus hovered above them and waited. Then he swooped down and snatched away the eye and the tooth, as one sister was passing them to another.

"Tell me where to find the Gorgons, or I will throw your eye and your tooth into the sea," he jeered.

Trembling with fear and anger the Grey Sisters gave Perseus his directions. Dropping their eye and their tooth onto the beach beside them, he flew on towards the Gorgons' lair.

Entering the dusky, twilight land where the monsters lived, Perseus saw around him still, grey figures of men and animals. One look into the eyes of the Gorgons had turned them to stone.

Perseus' blood ran cold within him. How could he succeed where so many others had failed?

At last Perseus found the Gorgons. They were asleep among the rocks, and Perseus was able to look at them safely.

Although they were asleep, the live serpents which formed their hair were writhing venomously. The sight filled Perseus with horror. How could he get near enough without being turned to stone?

Suddenly Perseus knew what to do. He now understood why Athena had given him the shining bronze shield. Looking into it he saw clearly the reflection of the Gorgons. Using the shield as a mirror, he crept forward. Then with a single swift blow he cut off the head of the nearest Gorgon. Her name was Medusa.

In one mighty swoop, Perseus grabbed the head of Medusa. He placed it safely in his bag and sprang into the air on his winged sandals.

As Perseus leapt into the air, the other two Gorgons came after him, screaming. The serpents on their heads hissed and writhed, and the Gorgons' wicked claws were outstretched to grasp him, but he was too quick for them.

The powerful wings on his sandals soon carried him out of their evil reach.

Their claws gripped the empty air behind his heels as Perseus flew to safety.

The two Gorgons turned to see the lifeless body of their sister, Medusa, lying on the ground.

As they watched, there sprang from her blood the white winged horse, Pegasus, the symbol of grace and beauty.

As Perseus passed over one of the islands he saw a strange sight. A young girl was standing chained to a rock beside the sea. Swiftly Perseus flew down and landed beside her. The girl was crying with fear.

"Who are you?" he asked, freeing her. "And who has chained you up like this?"

The girl was very frightened, but answered Perseus, "My name is Andromeda and my father placed me here. My mother boasted that I was more beautiful than the sea-nymphs, and the god of the sea, Poseidon, sent a sea monster to terrorise our island in punishment. The gods have told my father that the sea monster will only go away if I am sacrificed to it."

She cried bitterly as she told Perseus the story.

"Take my hand and we will fly from this monster," said Perseus.

Suddenly the girl pointed: "Look!" she screamed. "The monster!" Perseus turned and there was a huge beast coming out of the sea.

"Have no fear," the hero cried. "I have a weapon that no monster can withstand."

As he said this, he raised the Gorgon's head in the face of the monster. Instantly the beast was turned to stone.

So Perseus saved the life of Andromeda, and took her to Seriphos to be his wife.

When they came to Seriphos, Perseus went to the king's palace, for he had not forgotten Polydectes' villainy. He took with him the Gorgon's head, and found the king and his friends feasting.

They had no thought that Perseus would ever return.

When Perseus entered, Polydectes was annoyed. "What are you doing here?" he said with a scowl.

"I have kept my promise," said Perseus. "I have brought you a Gorgon's head."

Polydectes and his friends laughed. "You are lying," shouted the king. "No man could bring back a Gorgon's head."

Perseus pulled out the head and held it up
for all to see. "See for yourselves!" he cried.
Polydectes and his friends looked at the
head and at once were turned to stone.

Perseus gave back the gifts of the gods
and presented Athena with the Gorgon's
head to place upon her shield, in gratitude
for her help.

THE MAZE GAME

This is a maze rather like the one Theseus had to find his way throu
See if you can find your way to the Minotaur at the centre. The m
on this page has a number of different routes.